For Ella, in memory of May,
her grandmother – C. A. D.
For Lorna – R. R.

Barefoot Books
294 Banbury Road
Oxford, OX2 7ED

Text copyright © 2010 by Carol Ann Duffy
Illustrations copyright © 2010 by Rob Ryan
The moral rights of Carol Ann Duffy and Rob Ryan
have been asserted

First published in Great Britain in 2010 by Barefoot Books Ltd

This book has been printed in Italy
on 100% acid-free paper

Reproduction by B & P International, Hong Kong

This book was typeset in Twilight and Nordik
The illustrations were handcut from single sheets of paper,
individually coloured by spray paint and photographed

ISBN 978-1-84686-354-7

British Cataloguing-in-Publication Data:
a catalogue record for this book is
available from the British Library

5 7 9 8 6

THE GIFT

CAROL ANN DUFFY
AND
ROB RYAN

Barefoot Books
step inside a story

A LONG TIME AGO,

when the world and everything
in it was younger, there lived
a beautiful girl.

The girl lived in a small town with her mother and father. It was a quiet town, of a sort not found nowadays, and its sounds were church bells, children, cattle passing at the crossroads, boots on cobblestones, an accordion or a fiddle through the open window of an inn, the wordless voices of dogs, cats and, at night-time, owls.

Before she went to sleep, she would look out across the moon-oiled rooftops of the small town towards the dark wood at its edge, listening to the gentle query of an owl and wondering what her life would bring.

One day, in early summer, the girl
and her mother and father were
picnicking in the woods. The girl had started
to make a necklace of buttercups and daisies.
She wandered between the trees collecting her small
flowers. She reached a little clearing, where buttercups
sparkled in the sunlight.

The girl knelt to continue her chain of flowers. She
could hear the murmur of her parents' voices nearby
as she pierced neat slits with her thumb and fingernail
into the soft green stems of the buttercups.

Bees prayed for honey at a wild rose bush. A thought
suddenly came to the girl – as urgent and vivid as

a butterfly opening its orange wings – that she wanted
to be buried in this plot of land when she died.

No sooner had she had this strange, intense thought than there
was a rustle from the bushes and an old woman stood before her.
The woman, though lined with age and silver-haired, had a
strong and lovely face and her bright, watery eyes were kind. She
was barefooted and dressed in a long white robe.

'Give me your flower necklace,' she said to the girl, 'and you
shall have your wish.'
The girl was alarmed at this and got to her feet.
'What wish?' she said.
'The wish to be buried in this plot of land when you die.'
The girl stared as the old woman slowly sat down on the grass,
gazed up at her, and said again:
'Give me the necklace and you shall have your wish.'

The girl looked at the
chain of flowers in her hands.
Quickly, she made a final piercing and
joined the two ends of the necklace together.

Then she took three swift steps towards the old
woman and looped the necklace round her neck.
As she did this, the girl heard her mother's voice calling
her name and looked behind her – and when she
looked back again, the old woman was gone. The
girl turned and ran through the trees.

By the time the picnic was over, the girl had
started and finished another flower chain
and she said nothing to her parents
about the old woman.

Time passed slowly and the girl was often in the woods with her family or with her friends. Whenever she was there, she would wander off on her own and spend a few minutes in the little clearing. If she had found a special stone she would bring it to the clearing and place it there.

Once, she came with a pocketful of bulbs from home to plant – and they would be snowdrops. Another time, she came with a twist of paper with some seeds in and planted them. They would grow into forget-me-nots.

And as the girl grew into a young woman, the plot of land began to fill with the loveliest flowers, the most fragrant herbs, and the most perfect stones.

The young woman had art in her hands and she became a painter.
She had her own small house in the town now and worked there in
a room generous with light. In the evenings, she walked through
the town to her parents' house or to her friends' houses. She had
love in her heart and fell for a friend of a friend of a friend.

Soon enough she moved to a bigger house in the town with him.
She had a child in her belly and by the year's end she was a mother,
painting her pictures as her child slept in her cot next to the easel.
Time passed slowly and brought many people who wanted to buy a
painting. Another child was born.

The woman visited the woods many times with her children. She still went to the clearing and tended the plot of land as her children played hide-and-seek among the trees.

Sometimes she brought her paints and canvas and painted there and these paintings were amazing in their intense use of colour.

Time passed and one winter the woman's mother died and then her father. This was a season of real darkness for the woman. She painted nothing and kept her family close, as snow whirled and shredded itself around the house. But when spring came, she went again to the plot of land in the clearing in the woods, with a trowel and a screw of seeds.

The woman's life brought happiness in love and art and her children grew and flourished. In time, they moved to their own houses in the town and, before she knew it, the older woman was a grandmother.

She took her grandchildren for walks in the woods and when they gave her a special stone or a pebble, she made sure to take it to the clearing and place it there.

Time was passing quickly and soon she
had to walk everywhere with a stick. She stood at the
edge of the clearing, looking at the plot of land. She
knew all the names of the flowers – monkshood,
campion, stock, hollyhock, love-lies-bleeding,
snapdragon, columbine, cornflower, wallflower,

clematis, foxglove, sweet pea, flax, lupin,
honesty, marigold and rose of heaven. The air was
freighted with the scent of herbs – dill, chervil, borage,
sage, rosemary, angelica, camomile, wild garlic, hyssop,
lavender, tarragon and thyme. The stones and pebbles
shone in their patterns.

One day, even the stick could
not help the old woman to
walk and her new painting
lay unfinished on the easel.

She grew weak and her family
gathered round, talking quietly, and
her grandchildren drew pictures to
pin on the wall by her bedside.

The old woman felt no fear and told her family that, if anything happened, she wished to be buried in the plot of land in the clearing in the woods. She drifted into sleep and dreamed that she stood in the clearing again in her nightdress.

A young girl knelt there, making a chain of small flowers. She sat on the cool grass and the child stood up and stepped towards her to place the flower necklace around her neck.

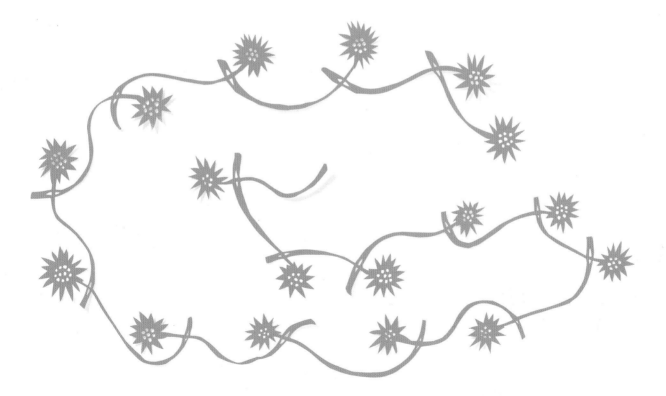

Her head filled with a sweet, golden light and as
she watched, the young girl turned and ran into
the juggling shadows of the trees.

Barefoot Books
step inside a story

At Barefoot Books, we celebrate art and story that opens the hearts
and minds of children from all walks of life, focusing on themes that
encourage independence of spirit, enthusiasm for learning and respect
for the world's diversity. The welfare of our children is dependent on
the welfare of the planet, so we source paper from sustainably managed
forests and constantly strive to reduce our environmental impact.
Playful, beautiful and created to last a lifetime, our products combine
the best of the present with the best of the past to educate our
children as the caretakers of tomorrow.

www.barefootbooks.com